THE KID WITH

THE
CAST IRON
STOMACH
DEE STERLING

"Nothing Comes to Sleepers, but a Dream"

This book would not be possible without
the guidance, patience and encouragement
of loved
ones and friends!

Thank you...

" The Kid
with
THE CAST IRON STOMACH"

DEE STERLING

Illustrations - Anibal Arroyo
Creative Imagery Flora Barber
Color Concepts—Flora Barber—Dee Sterling
Cover Design Concept - Dee Sterling - Anibal Arroyo
Cover Layout & Typeset Don S. McClure
Publication Consultation Don S. McClure
Caricature— Jeff Jackson

Copyright #T X u 8 6 6 2 4 5 Library of Congress
Copyright information:

Content

Chapter One: Yummy

Treamont Johnson was a fourth grader at

Grace Elementary School. Treamont was a boy
with a special talent, a very special talent indeed.
You see, Treamont was the only child in Grace
Elementary School that could eat a combination
of foods without ever getting a stomach
ache. Treamont's special recipes were so unique,
the other kids called him, The Kid with the "Cast
Iron" Stomach".

Every day at school the kids would form a circle
around Treamont and cheer him on as he ate
lunch. He would eat things such as apple sauce,
peanut butter and chocolate syrup all mixed
together.

One day however, Treamont went a bit too far. He made a gelatin, marshmallow, pickle, sardine and grape sandwich and topped it with mustard. This meal sent some kids running for the bathroom, but not Treamont. He laughed and washed it all down with a tall glass of orange juice. Treamont had three close friends. Their names were Olivia, Clark, and Marisha. Olivia, whom people sometimes referred to as "Comic Relief" because, of her smart comments, was wise and comical. Clark, was somewhat shy, but artistic and loyal. Then there was Marisha, honor student and "Fashion Police" The three of them had fun thinking up new dishes for Treamont to eat.

One morning as Treamont and Clark arrived at school, they saw a big white sign with blue writing which read, "Create Your Own Junk Food Contest". The two boys stopped in their tracks as Treamont's eyes lit up, and he began to imagine the endless possibilities. He would create the ultimate junk food masterpiece and be sure to win. The two boys daydreamed for a while, and then continued on to class.

During recess the four friends joined together to discuss their plan of action. First things first, what type of food did the contest mean? Did it have to be the hot or cold kind, the crunchy or soft kind? Treamont didn't mind, he liked them all. Soon the friends had exhausted all the types of junk food and still were not sure what kind the contest was talking about. Marisha decided she would find out about the contest rules right after recess. The bell rang and the friends had to return to class, so they agreed to meet up again at lunchtime.

Lunchtime arrived, and the first person to show up was Marisha. She had a peanut butter on wheat in one hand and the contest rules in the other.

Clark had turkey on white and Olivia had bologna and mustard on a roll; and of course there was Treamont, whom no one could ever be sure of what he would bring. Today was no exception, as Treamont brought his usual dinosaur lunch box with his unusual food. The circle began to form, as one by one, the items in his lunch box were unpacked. There was a thermos full of chicken and rice mixed with ketchup, onions, peas, relish and leftover pizza; for dessert, chocolate chip cookies and steak sauce! Clark's eyes widened, Olivia took out her camera and Marisha passed him a napkin. The other kids watched in amazement and asked him if he was going to enter the junk food contest. He grinned and asked Marisha, "What do the rules say?"

Marisha picked up the paper and began to read: "This contest is for Grace Elementary, Marshall Elementary and Stuart Elementary; which means you will have to compete with other students from different schools. It doesn't matter what type of junk food you choose, as long as it is original and you are able to consume it all.

There will be three judges and the contest will take place at Grace Elementary School auditorium on June 17th at three o' clock in the afternoon. There will be three prizes: 1st Prize-Five tickets to "Wonder World" (The Amusement Park of the Future) 2nd Prize- Three tickets to "Wonder World", and the 3rd Prize-A motorized "Mr. Chew" gumball machine."

The friends gleamed with Joy as they pictured themselves spending the whole day in marvelous "Wonder World".

There was no turning back now: they had to win that contest and win big! They decided to meet in the library at 7pm to brainstorm. Marisha went home and dug up her mom's recipe books. Treamont and Clark went to the library, and Olivia called her grandmother, who was a chef. Seven o'clock came and the four friends met to reveal their findings.

They each had such great ideas that they couldn't choose just one, so they combined lists and came up with the most ingenious creation yet:
The World's Biggest and Best Ice Cream Sundae!

Chapter Two: "Treamont's Bootcamp"

There were only two days left before the contest, so Treamont went into binge training. He had seen the movie "Rocky" a couple of times, so he knew what he had to do. He went home and raided his closet; he came upon his gym trunks and his lucky purple socks. Last but not least, he pulled out his cherished "Treamont Only" box and blew off more than one inch of dust.

He then dug under his treasured baseball trading cards and found his precious yellow dump truck. He lifted up the truck, popped open the back, and found his beloved, always worn, never washed, "Treamont's Triumphs" T-shirt, with the everlasting mustard and maple syrup stain.

He had achieved it at the "Hot-Dogs and Beans Tournament."

He was now ready to begin...

He ran to the garage and shut the door. This would be his secret mission. He bench-pressed potato chips, clean jerked chocolate bars, and slam-dunked doughnuts. He did so well, he impressed himself!

Chapter Three: "Super Spectacular Day"

On the day of the contest, the sun was shining. The sky was bluer than blue and the birds were singing. Treamont was readier than ready; nothing could bring him down today! He decided to forego lunch to prepare for the afternoon ahead. As Treamont walked into the school yard, he could see the other kids giving him the thumbs-up for encouragement.

During social studies, Treamont could not stop watching the clock. He was nervous and excited all at the same time. Finally, the bell rang and he made a mad dash for home. When he reached his house, he headed straight for his bedroom to dress. He had special clothes picked out for this event.

Olivia and Marisha were the first to arrive to set-up, and they each had a bag filled with ingredients. There were two other contestants setting up also. Clark got there shortly after, carrying a rather large box. The friends began to unload their groceries.

Chapter Four: "Treamont's Big Entrance"

At last, Treamont appeared. He had a bib and large spoon in his hand and looked very hungry. When the friends saw Treamont, their mouths dropped and they immediately looked at one another. Olivia glanced over Treamont from head to toe and boldly asked, "Treamont, you do have lights and mirrors in your house, don't you? Treamont replied, "Cool outfit isn't it?" Bravely, Clark stepped up and said "Well, I was just wondering if that was a hole in your sneaker or a window for your toes to see through?" Marisha folded her arms, tilted her head and asked, "At any time Treamont, did it ever cross your mind, that a blue checkered shirt and red vest should not be matched with a pair of stripped pea green pants, or is it just me?"

Treamont laughed and lifted his left pant leg to reveal his bright purple socks.

Chapter Five: "A Life of Their Own"

Upon revealing his purple socks, the wind blew, and the kids noticed a strange odor. They began to sniff around and ask, "What is that smell?" Treamont smiled triumphantly and said, "Oh, that smell?

That's me, I'm wearing my lucky purple socks; yep I haven't washed them in eight days for good luck!!" The friends could not believe their ears and stared at Treamont for a moment in disbelief. They soon went back to setting up for the contest, even though they kept their distance from him.

Chapter Six: "Everything & The Kitchen Sink"

The rival contestants for the contest were a boy named Jack Crump and a girl named Taylor Gleason. Jack was a small-framed boy with very little muscle. He was plainly dressed and wore thin, silver framed glasses. Taylor was quite chunky and had a lot of hair, which she wore in over-sized pigtails. She had on a flowered pink dress. The visitors could not help but notice the odd outfit Treamont was sporting. The crowd slowly started filtering in and soon the three judges were in place.

Principal Stone stood up and called everyone to attention. The principal began to tell the rules of the contest: "Thank you all for coming to the first 'Create Your Own Junk Food' competition. The rules are simple. The type of junk food can be any kind you want it to be, as long as you made it up yourself and you are able to eat it all.

The person with the most original entry wins! We have the school nurse, Mrs. Wimpole, standing by in case anyone needs her.

Everyone had their eyes glued on the tables. Jack Crump had invented, "The Everything Pretzel". It was a great big soft baked pretzel with cheese, bacon, hot-dogs and mustard in it! Very interesting! Then there was Taylor Gleason who had invented the, "Crunch Perfection" sandwich. This sandwich had bbq-corn chips, potato chips, pretzel sticks, popcorn, cheesy curls, sesame sticks and for that touch of sugar, sugar sticks! She used a buttered whole wheat roll for nutritional value. Finally, the entry the whole school had been waiting for: Treamont's "Kitchen-Sink" sundae.

There it was, a big blue bowl the size of a kitchen sink, loaded with chocolate, vanilla, butter pecan and strawberry ice cream. That was only the beginning. It was covered with chocolate chewies, peanut butter crunchies, fruit wraps, marshmallows, bubble gum, chocolate bars, nuts, granola, cream cakes, gum drops, peanut butter, cereal squares, mini cookies, and to round it off, chocolate syrup, and a mountain of whipped cream topped off with a dainty little cherry! The judges and the audience were drooling.

Principal Stone finished with, "By the wave of My hand, let the contest begin" The bell rang and the contest began. Jack had brought along a butter knife for his pretzel and was doing a good job of stuffing it down.

Taylor was sitting there, just eyeing her sandwich as if it were going to move, and all she kept mumbling was, "I can't believe I have to eat the whole thing" She looked a bit green. Taylor took one bite and headed for the restroom. The nurse followed her. Then, there was Treamont, sitting in front of what looked like a snowy Mt. Everest.

He did not use a normal spoon. That would be too conventional. No, he had to use a serving spoon from his mom's best table setting; he knew she would approve.

The sundae was disappearing rather fast, and the judges were on the edges of their seats. The crowd was cheering loudly. Jack gallantly gave up his struggle, short of his last bite of pretzel. Meanwhile; Treamont was leaning over his bowl and shoveling in the gigantic dessert. It didn't matter to him that everyone had now given up. He wanted to win big and live up to his name. Plus, he was starving!

Time ticked by and Treamont was coming up on his last mouthful. The crowd held their breath as Treamont opened his jaws to inhale the remaining spoonful. Suddenly, the spoon dropped into the empty bowl and Treamont rose to his feet, with his hands held high he did his dance of victory. The crowd's silence turned to cheers and applause.

Marisha, Clark and Olivia ran to his side and hugged him for a moment; soon they remembered his lucky purple socks and stepped back. They were proud of their friend, but couldn't help thinking about that first place prize to "Wonder World" (The Amusement Park of the Future)

Chapter Seven: "The Smell"

Principal Stone took the microphone again and began to speak. "This has truly been a competition of huge portions, and I am pleased to see the creativity and persistence the students here gave it. It is unfortunate; however, that Miss Taylor Gleason took ill and is now resting in the nurse's office. I want you all to know that you are all winners here today because of your willingness to participate."

Just as he was finishing his speech, the Assistant Principal walked over, handed him a piece of paper and left the stage. "Okay, the judges decisions are in" he said.

"The third prize goes to Taylor Gleason, of Stuart Elementary. "We do hope she will enjoy that motorized "Mr. Chew" gumball machine." Taylor was still resting in the nurses office, so Nurse Wimpole accepted her prize for her.

"The second prize goes to Jack Crump of Marshall Elementary, for his "Everything Pretzel", very impressive. "Enjoy your three tickets to "Wonder World", (The Amusement Park of the Future)". Jack came up on stage and eagerly accepted his prize.

"And the first prize goes to Grace Elementary's own, Treamont Johnson, for his unusual yet totally unique, "Kitchen-Sink" sundae. That was truly an extraordinary delight. Treamont will receive five tickets to "Wonder World", (The Amusement Park of the Future), and a trophy".

"Treamont, how did you come up with such a filling sundae?" Treamont wiped his chin and took the microphone. "Well, I figured since my mom is always telling me I eat everything except the kitchen sink, I'd prove her wrong! Might I add sir, it was delicious!"

With that comment said, Treamont let out a large belch of satisfaction. The crowd roared with laughter. Jack came over to congratulate him on his win.

Principal Stone ended with, "Treamont, you have fun at "Wonder World" with your friends, okay? And please, wear some new clothes!!! Well, this concludes the contest, thank you all for coming. We ask that you please not loiter around the school property, but, pick up all your trash and go directly home and do your homework". As he was leaving, Principal Stone noticed a strange odor and winced. "What's that smell?", he said, with his eyes half closed. Treamont kept quiet this time.

The End

With a captivating personal style, Dee Sterling, showcases her unique imagination. This fascinating new writer is a home-grown New Jersey girl. Simply put, this quirky and charming romp, based on her real-life brother, is a throw back to the old-school days of childhood, pure and simple.

"The Kid with the cast Iron Stomach"

Treamont Johnson doesn't just love to eat. He loves to create! Every one of his dishes are masterpieces in his eyes. One of Treamont's favorite snacks is chocolate chip cookies and steak sauce! Most people's stomachs would turn upside down hearing that, but not Treamont, he just smiles, chews and rubs his tummy!

Treamont not only has fun with his friends, but he fun with his food.
He is on his way to becoming the greatest "Foodologist" in the world, by his own standards!

Treamont is loosely based on my real-life brother. The other characters that you'll encounter, are reflections of my niece and other children, from the day care in which I worked. I aged them a little and added fascinating and fun personalities. Step into Treamont Johnson's extraordinary everyday life, courtesy of the literary world's newest author, Dee Sterling.

The young and the young at heart will enjoy meeting Treamont and his multi-cultural group of friends. You'll laugh as this endearing little fellow eats his way through the story and into your heart! You'll find that this is a wonderful book worth reading time and time again.

Soon you'll be telling all your friends about this little gem of a story,

"The Kid with the Cast Iron Stomach"